Badlands

by Alyson Faye

Chapeltown Books

© Copyright 2018
Alyson Faye

The right of Alyson Faye to be identified as author of this work has been asserted by her in accordance with the Copyright, Designs and Patents Act 1988
All rights reserved

No parts of this publication may be reproduced, stored in a retrieval system, or transmitted in any form or by any means, electronic, mechanical, photocopying, recording or otherwise without prior permission of the copyright owner.

British Library Cataloguing in Publication Data

A Record of this Publication is available from the British Library

ISBN 978-1-910542-25-5

This edition published 2018 by Chapeltown Books
Manchester, England

All Chapeltown books are published on paper derived from sustainable resources.

Dedication

To my husband for his computing help and moral support. To my teenage son for listening to me go on about plots when he'd rather be gaming. To James Nash, poet and tutor of Otley WEA Writers group whose encouragement started me writing again. To the folks at the writing groups who've listened, offered feedback and support. To Gill James for giving me this opportunity. A big thank you to you all.

Contents

Dedication	5
Introduction to 'Badlands' by Alyson Faye	9
Darkness Falls	**10**
Children's Games	10
A Gift for Krampus	13
Mother Love	16
Nest of Bones	17
The Wake Up Call	19
Mermaid	20
All Hallows' Eve	21
The Adelphi	22
Shadow Worlds	**26**
Cathedral Crow	26
Belladonna	28
Shadow Thief	32
Mirror Man	36
Bouquet from Valletta	38
Each Other's World	40
Darkness Rising	**42**
Chestnuts for my Sweet	42
Doll Man	43
A Guy for the Children	45

Scarecrow — 46
Love thy Neighbour — 49
Snow Man — 50
Treasure Hunt — 51
Tomb Land — 52
The Last Walk — 55
Ride of a Lifetime — 56
Crowd Control — 60

Laughter in the Dark — 62
3D Audrey — 62
Peacocks — 65
Zombie Hunting — 67
Vinnie's Family — 69

Life Scenes — 70
Cannon Fodder — 70
Going Home — 72
No Home for Holly — 73
Bookworm — 75
Visiting Mum — 77
MISPER — 80

Epilogue — 82
Dames and Rain Slicked Streets — 82

Acknowledgements of prior publication for Flash Fiction pieces — 85

Introduction to 'Badlands' by Alyson Faye

'Badlands' is a collection of flash fiction pieces, from drabbles of 100 words to longer pieces up to 1000 words. Many have been published on line and in anthologies, and short-listed or been placed in competitions. They have all been written during the last three years. The oldest pair being 'Chestnuts for my Sweet' and 'A Guy for the Children'. Both written in the autumn.

Previously in the 1990's I had two books for children published, fistfuls of poetry for the small press magazines and short stories. However it was on joining a WEA class near Leeds in 2012 that I rediscovered my writing 'mojo' and the pleasure of writing micro stories or flash fiction. This was a new term and a new idea for me. I embraced it wholeheartedly and I found that I had a flair for brevity. I liked the way I could play with different genres and envision a whole tale in a nutshell.

My short shorts reflect my interest in ghost stories, history especially the Victorians, old movies, derelict buildings, real life issues such as homelessness and just the 'what if' factor of when a seemingly normal situation starts to tilt off centre, dangerously so.

Alyson Faye
June 2017

Darkness Falls

"Monsters are real, and ghosts are real too. They live inside us and sometimes they win."
Stephen King

Children's Games

I've lost track of how long they've been out there; waiting. I can't run any longer. My chest burns, the cuts on my legs and arms throb. One of them is infected I am sure. I just don't look at it any more. There is no point.

'Horsey horsey don't you stop.'

The voices whisper, cry out, taunt. From over there in those scrubby bushes, from high up on the wire fence, from behind me. They are all around me. I can see black shapes flitting, like ravens. Only ravens leave you alone.

'Come out, come out wherever you are.' Laughter trickling, like waves undulating.

The first stone hits my right cheek. I feel warmth as the blood trickles down. It's just another cut to add to the long list of my injuries. A coke can lands at my feet, a bottle splinters over my shoulder smacking down on the concrete. I am in their playground.

I wrap my tatty mac around me, shiver and wish I had not come here this evening. I had been to all the usual spots, but I was too late and they had been occupied. I'd had a couple of nights in hospital last month when I'd cut myself so badly I'd passed out and someone had called an ambulance. Best two nights I'd had in ages they were too. Warm bed, clean sheets, food and drink. Bliss.

We all know the old Schoolhouse and its yard are best avoided. But I'd run out of choices. I'd hoped they wouldn't be there that night. I had got it wrong.

'Ring a ring a roses.'

The shadows leap and dance in a circle, overlapping. Fluttering like scraps of paper.

'All fall down.'

Screams of laughter. The shadows slip into the ground and slide away.

I start to recite the only protection I can think of, which I learnt as a child from my mother, long gone now. God rest her soul. She did her best.

'Our father who art in Heaven…'

Another missile hits me, a glancing blow. I shrug it off. Try and act tough. I want to make myself as small as possible so I curl up in a ball.

'Bloody little monsters,' I whisper. 'Go away!' Each breath hurts. My teeth ache profoundly. My vision blurs then clears. I pray not to pass out. Not here, in this place.

'Jack be nimble, Jack be quick.' They are urging me on. They want me to play with them.

They are a solid mass approaching me. Slowly they take shape. Some are dressed in jeans, others in pinafores, some in nightdresses. The youngest is sucking a grubby thumb. She's just a toddler. She seems so innocent. Their laughing dies. Silence falls. They all watch me. Will I run? Or am I done?

'Run rabbit run.'

They sing with such hope shining out of their faces, their eyes glinting in the moonlight. I shake my head. I smell the spark in the air, before I see it, crackling out from their midst. They all gasp and watch it snake its way towards me in my newspaper lined coat. The air is thick with smoke and glee. My prayers turn to ashes.

'Boys and girls come out to play…' The voices fade away. The shapes retreat in to the Schoolhouse, with its boarded up windows and signs reading 'Beware-Trespassers!'

A Gift for Krampus

Grunen Baum Platz during December was a gaudy sight. The gas lit lamps poured golden pools of light onto the pavement. Fir trees filled hallways laden with hundreds of lit candles. Tiny groups of carol singers darted from door to door, singing 'O Tannenbaum, O Tannenbaum.' Their reward: Gluhwein.

'Oh Papa, I love this time of year.' Emilie hugged her father.

'I know darling girl. This Krampusnacht will be particularly special.'

Emilie gazed up at her father's unsmiling face. He and Mama were so sad now. Ever since… Emilie's thoughts skittered away.

'St Nicholas will only come for good girls who are in bed asleep,' Jans Albrecht told her.

Snuggled in bed, buried under a pile of blankets Emilie prayed, 'I've been a good girl truly I have.'

In the basement Jans laboured on his daughter and her present. His thoughts returned to that summer morning when Emilie had raced into his study, 'Papa, come quickly! Lucia is hurt.'

Seeing how much blood there was on Emilie's dress, he'd followed her with foreboding to their orchard. There Jans had found his daughter Lucia lying among the windfalls. Blood leaking from her cranium.

He carried her body home and laid her out in the parlour. He could not let her leave him, though his wife had begged for a burial.

Jans did not blame Emilie. Her twin had always been the more daring, climbing trees like on that day or tormenting the neighbours.

The dreams had begun not long after. Dreams where Krampus roamed, so vividly lifelike, Jans believed he could hear the clanking of his chains.

Deprived of his rightful prize, the naughty Lucia, the demon promised to take Emilie as compensation on the upcoming Krampusnacht. After all, the demon insinuated, Emilie had been naughty too.

Jans touched the object lying on his workbench; the silky black hair, the crimson velvet of the dress, the wax face. The beautiful doll he'd moulded in Lucia's image. He was particularly proud of her eyes. He prayed that this creation would be enough to satisfy the demon the next evening.

Krampusnacht evening Emilie opened the beribboned box. 'She looks just like me Papa. Danke, danke.'

Emilie stroked the doll's face. Under her fingers the eyes opened.

'Look Papa. Her eyes are the same green as Lucia's.'

Jans smiled, 'I know. The very same.'

The parlour door crashed open, 'It's the Krampus!' Emilie screamed, cowering.

Krampus' horns scraped the edge of the chandelier, as he lumbered towards Emily. His hoofs left imprints on the Turkish rug. His hairy tail flicked out behind him. He bent towards Emilie and the Lucia doll. Jans held his breath. The demon's red lolling tongue could not be contained in his mouth. To Jans' disgust the demon licked Emilie's hair, then the doll's face. In seconds Krampus made his choice and departed.

Jans sank to the floor. He had saved Emilie. She was safe.

Emilie sat huddled, rocking herself, crooning 'Come back Lucia, come home.'

Mother Love

Edward suspects his mama is mad. He has been thinking this more and more lately. Every afternoon mother and son withdraw to the parlour overlooking the ruins of the garden. Edward sits hunched, shoulder to shoulder with the pianoforte, jostled next to a ring of chairs arrayed for the guests. Guests who never come. Except for one who is not welcome.

The pile of black edged calling cards lie, like ravens' feathers, in the hallway. Papa has left for the City 'on business'. The servants are all departed. Even Nanny Mary, had finally given up. She'd left sobbing, kissing and hugging Edward to the last.

Mama sits every day in her black draperies, gazing at Edward's baby brother, Ernest.

'Do you think he looks a little pallid today?'

Silence fills the huge spaces in the room while Edward ponders a suitable reply.

Nodding sagely he answers, 'Yes, Mama. A little.'

Mama reaches over with her rouge to rub more colour into Ernest's flaccid cheeks.

Edward's baby brother rests, propped up against the red velvet cushions. He is pale as ice cream and might, in dim lighting, be mistaken for slumbering. Edward knows different.

The vicar is still striving to give Ernest a Christian burial.

Nest of Bones

The long low slung rooms under the eaves meander away. It is a maze up here of interconnected spaces hidden away from the house's inhabitants. I breath in the stagnant air, finger trace patterns in the half century old dust which smothers every surface. Sunlight streams in, fighting past the grime on the windowpanes. In its beams I watch dust motes dance. All is still.

A shadow flits by the right hand side window, I jump. Another follows, swooping under the eaves.

'Birds. Of course.' I breathe out. They'll have a nest under there I decide.

Looking away towards the huge metal trunks, I hear a CRACK! The tinkling of broken glass makes me turn around.

The window is now crazily shattered, with tiny shards flying around and there lying on the floorboards a brown feathery ball. Despoiled. The bird's blood spatters in the dust. It is an obscene sprinkling of red. Its wings are tattered.

The air in the room rushes out through the newly made hole as if the room's soul is escaping. Both repulsed but compelled to tidy up, I inch towards the bird. It twitches and I yelp, leaping back into a chest of drawers and hitting my spine.

A fly lands on the bird's glassy eye. It does not blink. Sickened I turn away. In the dead ashy fireplace a nest lies. A tangle of dried twigs and dead grasses intricately interwoven. It must have fallen down the chimney.

Inside it nestles delicate white bones. Cuddled up together. I hold them in the palm of my hand. Behind me I hear thump after thump becoming ever more frantic. Turning I see bird after bird, a sparrow, a blackbird and a largish crow fly directly into the attic windows.

Some of the birds succeed in breaching the hole in the glass; others reel away. I cower behind a wardrobe, terrified at this avian onslaught.

The birds that make it through flap around drunkenly. Then they land, often lying on their sides. In desperation I fling the nest of bones in their direction. I'm compelled to do this but don't understand why.

A sparrow picks up one of the bones in its beak, a wren picks up another. A chaffinch another. A raven carries the skull away. Away they fly out of the broken attic window with their bone booty. Leaving in their wake, broken glass, a few feathers and me, huddled terrified behind a horsehair settee.

The Wake Up Call

I was on the run. From her, the kids and my old life. I landed up in a rather grimy hotel on the north Norfolk coast, drawn there by memories of childhood holidays. I decided to book a coach trip with an outfit called 'Pioneer' (that was me now), requested a wake-up call from the blue haired girl on reception, hit the bar and then my bed. I slept like the dead.

The phone rang, 'It's time Sir.'

Jarred half awake, I answered, 'Huh? What?'

'Your time sir. It's come.'

Disorientated, I staggered up, caught my foot on the rug, tripped and fell into the carpet's embrace.

Where I stayed for hours. Out like a light.

Emerging at dinner the receptionist apologised. She'd forgotten to call my room.

Shrugging it off, I took the local paper from her and read 'Pioneer Coach Crash on A11, 5 Dead.'

Mermaid

He put her in a glass tank, full of water and watched her every day. He knew he had to wait. He did not know how long the waiting would last.

Every day the lady of the sea became thinner, her hair less glossy, her tail scales lost their lustre and her coral nails chipped away as she beat on the glass walls of her prison.

Her wailing kept Gabe and his wife awake, but since they'd lost their youngest lad at sea one stormy night, they didn't sleep much anyway.

Seven nights later, while the wind whipped frantically outside their cottage walls, a fierce knocking at their door fetched Gabe out of his bed.

On the doorstep stood their youngest lad, dripping wet and stinking of the sea.

Slurring he spoke, 'I've come for my wife.'

Gabe glanced at his son's ring finger where nestled, a coil of scales looped with a wisp of hair.

'I've been holding her for you son,' Gabe said. 'So your Ma could get to say her goodbyes.'

The revenant turned drowned eyes on his mother, he dribbled sea water from his mouth.

There was nothing left of her boy. His mermaid bride owned him now.

All Hallows' Eve

We gorge ourselves on the scents and sounds of the street market. Rows of pumpkin heads leer at us, pyramids of witches' hats threaten to topple over, a skeleton busker dances a jig, everywhere tiny ghouls and demons run around. We smile indulgently at their antics. They are so innocent, so.... unaware. They do not notice us.

From behind the church we hear the notes of a lone pipe. Lured over, we make our way through the long grass entwined around the tombstones. Among them shadows flit. You tug at my hand, eager to join them.

A child steps forward, bedraggled, unkempt with huge dark eyes. She beckons and ventures a small smile, showing rotted teeth.

Repelled I step away but you do not. You take the girl's bony hand. The music soars and I know you cannot resist. Not on this night. When the dead roam and come calling. I have to let you go.

Selfishly, I have kept you with me, chained by my love. You will always be my soul mate. My own Eve.

The Adelphi

It's not easy being the youngest. Becca was always being left out or left behind. It wasn't fair. She so wanted to be in. Especially with them. So when Jake and Joss had laughingly challenged everyone to the 'hugest dare ever,' Becca had been the first in the gang to leap up and accept. Now she was sorry. Sorry seven times over. Joss had nearly choked on her chewing gum. Jake had smirked behind his usual fag.

'OK Titch,' he'd said. 'You're on.'

Then he had bent down and whispered into Becca's ear. Her bones had melted and she'd had to hold onto her bladder. 'Bastards!' which was about the worst word she could think of.

Two nights later she crept out of her family's tiny terraced house, with its clutchy curtains, and began hiking out of town on its main road.

'We 'll know if you bottle it Titch,' Jake had said.

She saw him watching her from his bedroom window when she went past his parent's house. Keeping his beady on her. She waved gaily to show him.

The old Adelphi was derelict. Which didn't stop kids, druggies and the homeless creeping inside its rotten shell. Looking up Becca felt dwarfed. It had been such a grand old behemoth, with statues of lions on either side of the front door.

Bollocks, she thought.

'Don't forget Titch, you gotta go right inside. All the way down to the basement, take a photo and send it me,' Jake had instructed, smiling all the time. As if he was her mate.

Becca knew how to get in; knew exactly where to lift the broken hoardings and slide through, only leaving a little bit of skin behind.

Inside she stood in the Adelphi's ballroom. Once a vast marble floored space; now rubble strewn, filthy and seriously echoey.

Her phone bleeped. It was Joss, 'You there yet girl?'

Becca frowned but obediently texted back, 'Yeah. In ballroom. Stinks.'

Joss sent an emoji of a smiley face, 'Mind the dead bodies.'

'Cow,' muttered Becca. But she didn't text that back.

In the shattered wall mirrors she caught a glimpse of movement. She swung around sharply.

'Who's there?' The glass shards crunched under her trainers.

No reply. Just my imagination, she thought.

In the foyer a trapped sparrow was frantically beating its wings against the ceiling's fabulous plasterwork. The door leading to the basement was swinging slightly on its hinges. Just as if someone had gone through it. Becca gulped. That's where she had to go.

Reluctantly Becca pushed open the door and holding her breath because of the smell, she inched her way down the stairs. Past signs which read 'Kitchen' and 'Laundry'. Down, down, several flights until the 'Basement' sign greeted her.

'OK let's do this,' she encouraged herself. The carpet was mushy with mould. The walls splattered with greeny damp patches like a Pollock painting gone to seed.

Worst of all though Becca could feel an energy down here, a thrumming almost. Pushing open another corridor door she found herself staring at floor to ceiling wooden racks used for storage. She could hear scuttling. The air was a mix of wood, damp and something metallic.

'Just rats that's all girl. Chill,' she told herself.

She knew if she didn't get this pic, she'd be out, ostracised, tormented, hounded. Right now though, she thought, perhaps she could cope with all that.

Becca held up her iPhone and took the shot. In the momentary flash she glimpsed a figure hanging from one of the top racks, his feet jerking, doing the death dance. Legions of dark things appeared scuttling around on the ground feeding while a dark stain began to leak out from under the racks.

Becca turned and raced for the stairs. Heart thumping, bile in her throat, sweat pouring down her body. Adrenaline roaring through her system. In her haste to escape, she ripped her hand on the barbed wire fence. She knew she'd need to go to A&E the next day. Damn it.

Only when she was back in her own street, did she pause and take out her iPhone to check the image again. Surrounded by her neighbours' bins, gardens and under the street lamps she felt calmer.

The image she'd sent to Joss and Jake showed a cellar filled with tall wooden racks, stretching back into darkness. No hanging man, no scuttling insects, no stain. Except maybe just in the top right corner there was a black spot like a fly. Or something.

Hearing a rustle behind her Becca jerked around. No one was there. Except she thought she'd just missed seeing something scuttle away behind No 33's recycling bins. 'A rat, that's all it'll be,' she told herself firmly.

Tomorrow she'd go to A&E, tell Joss and Jake to shove it, 'cos they weren't anything like as scary as what she'd seen in the basement and she'd stay home more. 'Sorted,' then she muttered. 'I'm all sorted.'

Shadow Worlds

"All of life is a foreign country."

Jack Kerouac

Cathedral Crow

We were strolling around the cloisters when we first noticed the crow.

It was just perched on the stone wall with its head cocked. It seemed to be watching us.

A black garbed reminder of the legions of dead monks who'd prayed here.

'Shoo.' Mum flapped her hands at it.

Billy chucked a stone. Mum told him off. 'Show some respect.'

Wherever we walked in the cathedral grounds the crow came with us. An avian shadow.

It made me feel goose-bumpy and a bit sick. Billy of course made a game of it, talking about crow pie for tea.

We wandered inside to gaze at knights' tombs and jewel like stained glass windows. Which was when I remembered Grandma telling me years ago, 'The crows know.'

She'd been dead a little while by then. I had never really understood Gran's sayings.

The memory grew and ripened though. That night while our little household slept I went to her wooden chest and unearthed her cloak of feathers. It was an heirloom; the birds' plumages interwoven. Fabulously glossy light catchers.

The crow was waiting for me outside. I perched on the six foot garden wall, wrapped the avian mantle around me and took flight towards the cathedral spire.

It's a family tradition.

Belladonna

The children danced around the towering maypole, wrapping the brightly coloured ribbons in the time honoured routines they had been taught, creating fluid rainbows while they sang and laughed. Each child wore a fragrant hand woven garland (daisies for innocence). Each child shook a tin rattle packed with their baby teeth. The air was filled with the scents of burning herbs. Rosemary for remembrance; thyme for courage. It was an apparently joyous scene watched by the whole village.

The congregation cheered and clapped except for Missy who was white faced and taut lipped, standing on the edges of the group, set apart by her grief for her lost girl. The villagers shunned her, afraid to show sympathy. Their Pastor forbade open displays of mourning. He instructed his Flock to express only joy at the dying of one year and the birth of another. The lost ones he instructed them, were part of the price to be paid for the Flock's well-being.

There were, thought Missy, so many who were lost – to the plague which had decimated their village population; to the night demons who stole their animals under cover of darkness; to the forests where poisonous flora flourished. This was before you added in the ones nominated by the Pastor's cursed ballot box. She knew the elders gossiped at dusk around their hearths – of how to overthrow the Pastor, but no man it seemed would dare to stand against him.

A tiny child, skinny as a sparrow, clinging to her mother's roughly woven skirts, peeked out. Wide-eyed, innocent and ignorant. Her eyes are such a wondrous colour, thought Missy. Geranium blue. Though she likely will not survive the next three years. Young girls were frequently the chosen. The boys, less so. Missy suspected this was because they were needed to trap food, fight and labour. The Pastor's splendid dwelling had taken months of the men's toil.

Missy listened, head bowed, while the Pastor emoted with passion, spitting liberally as he thumped his fist on the table. He declared the dead girl's great sacrifice had been for the good of the Flock. His words were spiky thorns ripping into her chest. Her thoughts lay with her dead daughter who had been no more than eight harvests old when the Collectors arrived, bringing their hated nets and ropes. It had been like capturing a wild bird and breaking its wings.

Missy's scrawny, blue veined hand clutched at the freshly torn sprigs in her apron pocket. She had gathered them from the forest's mulchy guts the previous night. It was forbidden to do so but she was beyond caring. Sweet lush Belladonna; in honour of her lost girl.

The pastor finished with his usual blessing. It was time to curtsey and depart. Time to prepare. Her neighbours shuffled past her, caps in hand, eyes averted. Too afraid to speak. She had to free the village, let them be reborn again. Bring an end to the ballot box for the lost. Only the child with the geranium eyes stared openly at her. Missy boldly pointed to her apron pocket then slashed her throat with her forefinger. Wide eyed the child scurried away.

In her cottage she baked bread for the Pastor's supper as was the custom and fashioned the garland with her daughter's ribbons and hair. This would be laid in the Pastor's hearth. Her tears fell freely as she did this. They fell into the herbal drink she brewed to the time honoured recipe.

When the torches were lit outside Missy gathered up her basket of goodies and traversed the path to the Pastor's splendid abode where he lived alone. He was the only villager with that privilege. Families of up to thirteen or more, often crowded together into one small dwelling. So when plague descended whole families expired in a few nights. Missy had noticed this pattern and had pressed the elders to build more homes. The Pastor had vetoed this. As he did all change. Birth and death he intoned, were part of the natural cycle of life.

Missy knocked, waited and then entered, curtseying. A fire burned in the hearth, the floor was freshly swept and the air smelt of rosemary. She swung her basket up clumsily onto the table as it bounced against her swollen belly.

'Welcome my child.' The Pastor rose from the fireside chair. 'Come here.'

Missy tolerated his hand stroking her stomach and touching her face in a blessing. She felt the baby within turn and kick.

'Soon now Missy.' The Pastor smiled. 'You will be a mother again. As I promised you. You will no longer heed the one you lost.'

Missy closed her eyes and thought of her midnight foraging trip to the forest. Hate bubbled up in her but she pressed it down. She smiled instead as a dutiful Follower. In the corner of the room she espied the wooden ballot box with its pile of stacked counters.

The Pastor sat at the table and bent his head in prayer. Missy did the same. Then she began to lay out the bowls and bread in the required order. The jug with the herbal drink she placed at his right elbow.

'My beautiful Missy you have done all that is required.' The Pastor gazed at her belly while he took a generous swig.

The whole village turned out for the crowning of the Spring Queen. There was abundant ale drinking, dancing galore, while the ballot box burned superbly and a lamb was slaughtered for food and cooked over the coals. Missy cradled her new born daughter close to her chest in the woven sling.

'How is Bella this fine day?' asked her neighbour Mistress Lively.

'Flourishing. Thank ye.' Missy laughed.

The girl with geranium eyes, a skinny scrap, snuggled up and put her hand in Missy's apron.

Pulling out sweet treats, the girl did not eat them, but hesitating, dropped them to the mud.

Shadow Thief

The night light emitted a tiny glow. The shadow creeping across Lizzy's bedroom wall swallowed it. Lizzy hid under the covers. What would it take from her tonight? Last night it had stolen her toes. She had managed to hide that from her mum by keeping her shoes on all day.

Giant shadow fingers, thick as tar, stroked her face, then her lips. Next morning Lizzy couldn't speak. Her mum touched Lizzy's dumb lips gently.

'Don't be afraid. I can help you my love.'

Her mum gave Lizzy a huge vanilla scented drawing pad and a twiggy bunch of charcoal sticks.

'Draw it please. We call it a Shadow Thief. They steal parts of sleeping children at night for their own uses. They need your voice to talk in their world you see.'

Lizzy felt a surge of relief. Her mum believed her. It was not just all in her head as she had feared. She never questioned how her mother knew about such things although she understood her mother was not like her school friends' mothers. The ones who scrabbled at their iPhones, gossiped like squawking gulls at the school gates and baked immaculate cakes.

True her mum did make a lot of stuff at home and while some of her creations sold on Etsy, there were others Lizzy knew, which had to be kept secret. The willow web was one of those.

Lizzy and her mother set out to harvest the willow from the nearby park, early at dawn. The wood was dew soaked and really bendy. At home her mum sat down by the kitchen table, firmly grasped the willow wands and gently wove them into an intricate web, twisting it into patterns with deftness and skill. She sang while she did this. Strange, ancient words that Lizzy didn't understand but which made her feel safe.

'It's to bless the willow and make it more powerful,' her mum explained.

Lizzy only knew she couldn't get her voice back without help and that she was growing weaker while this shadow creature was becoming stronger.

She wrote on her pad, 'Web. Cool.'

Her mum smiled. 'Now we need just two more extras to give it powers.'

She grabbed Lizzy's hand mirror and smashed the glass carefully into a bowl. Lizzy gasped soundlessly. The tiny shards glimmered and reflected her face, broken and shattered. It was how she felt inside as well.

'We must weave glass pieces into the web,' her mum added.

She pulled open the fridge door and pulled out a container filled with brown rusty fluid. Her secret stash, as she liked to joke. Lizzy shuddered. She knew what it was. Plucking the hair ribbon from Lizzy's head, her mum dip-dyed it in the brown liquid. The pigs' blood slowly stained the blue satin ribbon which had some of Lizzy's hair attached to it.

'Yuk!' She mouthed silently.

Her mum laughed, 'You won't be saying that later on. You'll be grateful I'm doing this.'

She wrapped the blood stained ribbon around the willow web.

'There. Let it dry now. We'll hang it in your bedroom window this evening.'

At bedtime Lizzy settled down under her duvet while her mum sat cross-legged on the beanbag beside her. The willow web was tied in place across the window.

'I'll read you a story Lizzy.' Her mum picked up a battered copy of Grimm's Fairy Tales, an old favourite.

'They knew a thing or two about us, did those Brothers Grimm.' Her mum laughed. 'But they didn't know everything.'

Lizzy listened to her mum's soothing voice and watched her lunar clock tick off the minutes. She felt warm, cosy and safe. She drifted off but woke with a start. It was one in the morning.

'Shush,' her mum whispered, pointing at the window.

The web was stretching inwards, creaking and bending. Behind it a shadowy figure pushed against the willow. Its long black inky arms reaching through the web were grabbing at the air and fighting to gain entry. The web held firm. The shape scrabbled with long inky fingers, then sniffed the blood soaked ribbon; it recoiled as if in horror.

Her mum stood up tall, 'Get thee gone yonder Shadow Thief. You will take nothing more from my child.'

Her mum spoke a few words in an exotic other worldly language Lizzy didn't understand, but she knew they were definitely not French. The windowpane cracked but the web held firm. The glass pieces entwined in the willow web cut away parts of the Shadow Thief's arms. The dark blobs fell to the floor and the Shadow Thief gave a roar that Lizzy could feel through her skin. The web vibrated furiously, the ribbon ripped away, flying out into the night.

Lizzy grabbed her throat and spat out gunky black spittle onto the long suffering carpet. It lay there wriggling.

'Mum. Thank you.' Lizzy burst into tears. Her tears fell onto the black gunk and it withered away. Inside her bed socks her reclaimed toes wriggled.

'It's gone for good I promise you my love.' Her mum put her arms around Lizzy. 'Same thing happened to me about your age. Your Grandma sorted it for me. She was one of the best. So very very talented. She could have taught those Grimm Brothers a thing or two.'

Mirror Man

I wanted to escape. I drove and drove until the huge bridge which divides north from south was behind me. I booked into a drab little establishment. It lay in the shadow of the Humbers which suited my mood. Those ancient rotting ships' hulks were overflowing with gory legends.

I booked a boat trip to explore the ships' carcasses. Drinking heavily, sodden with self-pity and whiskey I fell on top of the bed and slept. The phone rang. Disorientated, I reached out for it, but it was not there. The ringing seemed now to be resonating from the other side of the wall.

It didn't stop and no one answered it. Now wide awake, I frantically pressed my hand to the wallpaper with its satiny flowers – with only one thought. To make the noise stop. The shrill ringing peeled away layers of my skin. Flakes shed onto the carpet, lying there like rime.

Stumbling to my feet, I rushed out into the corridor and hammered on the door of my neighbour. It swung open under my barrage. Stepping inside I realised the room was a mirror image of my own. It had its own occupant too. A man, my age and build; asleep under the bedclothes.

I went to shake his shoulder.

'Hey Mister. How can you sleep through that infernal ringing?'

The words seeped like sludge from my lips and dribbled onto the carpet. The man didn't respond.

I tried to pick up his phone, but my fingers slid across the handset like water. I could not get a grip.

Not on anything it seemed. I half slid, half lurched across the carpet and caught a horrifying glimpse of myself in the mirror.

Where was the real Jay? Pressing my hand against the window pane, I could feel nothing and my palm left no mark. The man behind me in the bed stirred finally and answered the phone. I heard a tinny voice through the receiver.

'Your time sir. It's come.'

The man got up, slipped on the rug and fell, hitting his head on the bedside cabinet. He lay unconscious, as if reclaimed by sleep. I peered into his face. He did look the image of me, albeit a younger happier version. I eased my way out of the room and continued to slither like a thin grey shadow from room to room, along corridors and through gaping doorways.

The Humbers pulled at me, with all their secrets. I could hear the ghosts' whisperings that day – so clear and so near. I climbed into the biggest ship's hulk; sailed it into the rough waves. I drank salt water and sky all day. I felt so alive.

Returning late at night to my room no one noticed me. The other Jay still lay on the floor, slowly bleeding out from a head wound. I tried to staunch it, but could not. My hand would not keep its shape. I dreamt of my day out sailing, where I was so free. I wanted to stay that way forever.

Bouquet from Valletta

'My darling Jack, I had to get away. Don't think of this as an ending, because I hope for me there will be a rebirth. Each spring. You will come to understand. I have seen too much here. Valletta has opened its maw, shown me its marrow. It has been decided for me you see. Taken out of my hands.

If only you could have seen these streets of Neapolitan ice cream coloured houses! Valletta is edible. At first, I was like a beggar at a banquet. All its orifices were closed to me. I was happy just to wander daily within the town's corkscrew heart. But secretly I craved more. More of its heart. Its offal.

Miraculously, on my sixth day here, one door cracked ajar. Exposing in its innards, a fantasia of flora, in cartoon colours, tangling and tumbling. I had an 'Alice in Wonderland' moment, falling, falling. Then the door slammed shut. I wept. Strangers stared, hurried by.

Tantalised, hooked now, like an addict, I was lured back. On the tenth evening, stumbling along and yes, my love, booze-soaked, as usual, I halted outside that same door. Its sudden opening took us both by surprise. Me and him. The garden man. He gleamed sweatily. Glancing down I remember thinking his hands were covered with rose petals.

Fuzzy-footed, I swayed and involuntarily, grabbed his hand. Felt the sticky, cloying texture on his flesh. Looking up I met his eyes. Obsidian chips. His fingers flexed and curled. I watched fascinated. Powerless.

I was dragged roughly through the aperture. Joy flowered in me. This is what I had always wanted. To be on the inside. To be accepted. To be part of something bigger.

I rest now, behind the high ochre coloured walls. Cosy and so snug. Bundled up against the largest hibiscus. Its florid petals cover my damaged head, which has leaked into the earth. Releasing its precious fluids. I float. I dream. I am comfortable, at peace. This soil is rich and is regularly nourished. More will join me in time. I will put down roots here. I will flourish.'

Each Other's World

Millie stepped outside, mask in place, clutching her dolly. Little Joe watched her from the windows of their house. She sidestepped the oily, viscous puddles which decorated the pavement. If anyone else had been watching she looked as if she was skipping along to a party. Except for her lank unwashed hair and torn clothing.

When their ma had gone away, she had left Millie in charge. There had been no one else left.

'Someone will come and save you,' she'd promised.

They had believed her then. They were still waiting. The kitchen larder was emptying. Provisions were scarce; clean water was a problem. You had to find other liquids to drink.

Joe could see their cul-de-sac was strewn with wrecked cars, dead pets and seeming piles of rubbish from which arms and legs protruded. He gulped and felt that lump in his throat again. He must not cry. It was a waste of water.

A man strolled into view. A grown up. Joe couldn't remember the last time he'd seen an adult. Well, an adult he felt safe with. Perhaps Joe hoped, perhaps this man would be different.

Joe watched Millie duck down behind the burned out carcass of a car. Hiding herself. Waiting to see what the man did next. There were the good things he might do or the other things.

The man stumbled. He looked like a scarecrow, rake thin. His lips and skin were chapped and raw. Millie could see those details from her hiding place. It was not looking too good she thought. He dropped to the ground, onto his knees, as if praying and then he began to lap up the oily puddles. Like an animal at a water pool. Millie kept on watching. Even though she didn't want to. In a minute or slightly less, the man's head reared back and he began to change. Spewing black viscous gunk from his mouth. Just like all the others she'd seen on the TV and in their cul-de-sac and in the streets round and about.

She hoped Little Joe had abandoned his viewing spot at the window. His nightmares were bad enough already. They only had each other. They were each other's world.

Darkness Rising

"You ever get the feeling all hell's about to break loose and there's nothing you can do about it?"
Ali Vali, The Devil Unleashed

Chestnuts for my Sweet

Ravenous, we split them open. They lie naked, exposed. They've already been ripped off the branch, then tortured by burning, finally brown bagged.

Greedily we devour them. Pete and me, warming our hands first. We tongue test the heat of their crunchy guts. We're laughing, together. Pete can't resist, he chucks one at me. It catches my cheek. Makes the hidden bruise there flare.

I wince, but giggle, as I return his fire. I didn't expect a bull's eye. Not at my first attempt. I got him in one, on his left temple. He went down hard, with a look of surprise on his face. Blood trickles into his eye. He does not blink.

He was lucky. I always knew what was coming. Just never always knew the when.

I sob and say to anyone who'll listen, 'It was just a silly game. That's all.'

Doll Man

'Mummy! Look what I've found!'

Amy tugs impatiently at her mum's sleeve, while Janey taps on her iPhone.

'In a minute. Just let me finish.'

Amy shrugs, skips back to her 'discovery', pokes it then pulls at the filthy trousered leg. It jerks. The white plastic bag, wrapped around the bony fingers, floats upwards. Tugging to escape, in the skin slicing January winds.

Amy, pink-cheeked, rearranges the man's fingers, so he can better hold the cup of tea she pretends to present to her 'guest.'

'Nice cup of tea Mister. That'll warm you up.'

She's noticed how cold the man's hand feels. 'Proper chilled.' As her Nan would say.

'Nippy at this time of year Mister.' Amy parrots the words Janey had tossed at the neighbour earlier.

'Here's my scarf.'

She unwraps her fleecy scarf, carefully wrapping it around the man's neck, like her mum does for her. Amy pats his shoulder. 'That'll warm you up.'

She wonders what else she might do to help. Regretfully she peels off her furry red mittens, a gift from her Nan. Nan's always saying it's good to help others.

Amy gently pulls the man's dirty fingers into her mittens. Her eye falls on the undone laces of his solo trainer.

'I'm not very good at laces, but Mummy says I need to practise more.'

Amy pokes out her tongue, concentrating. '...over and under... one loop... oops, nearly...' she mutters.

Her guest wears a cap which covers the top half of his face. Amy can only see his lips. They look blue. It seems rude to lift his cap when he's having a sleep, but she really wants to see his eyes. He hasn't moved at all. Trying to be bold, Amy reaches out towards the cap's brim.

'Come on Amy it's time to go.' Janey shouts.

Amy hovers, uncertain, then pats his shoulder instead.

'Bye Mister. See you tomorrow.'

She crawls out from under the slide, turning her face towards her Mummy, she waves happily. Mittenless.

Only the plastic bag bobs a goodbye.

A Guy for the Children

Fear coats me like a second skin.

'Remember remember the 5th November…'

The kids shriek the old rhyme while they leg it 'round the playground, chucking cans, stones, even dirt at me. Huddled, shivering inside my tatty raincoat, I rock myself for comfort.

'Go away,' I whisper.

It's dark. Late. I wish I had somewhere else to be.

Their shadows flit in and out of the swings and climbing frame, looping, swirling. Like ravens.

Their hands ablaze with sparklers, thrusting at me.

'Run!' one shouts.

'Jump!' screams another.

The newspapers around me burst into flames.

I will be headlines.

Scarecrow

They'd heard the bombers going over head, but they knew they were aiming for the cities. So Harry, his younger brother Jake and their mum did what they always did – they went to their beds in the farmhouse. They'd all been up since 5 o'clock that morning and as usual they were exhausted. Harry didn't even bother changing into his pyjamas, though he knew his mum would tell him off for that small omission in the morning.

The farm and its accompanying land was sizeable and there was only the three of them left to keep it going. Every day the trio of land girls arrived and they worked hard, but still it was a skeleton team compared to before the war.

Harry whispered his nightly prayer for his father, making sure he didn't disturb Jake and then he let the black wave of sleep consume him.

At dawn Harry was up first. He fed the chickens, cleaned out the pig sty, milked the cows and only then while pausing for a break, did he glance northwards towards their largest field.

'That's damn odd,' he muttered. 'Wonder why he's all lopsided like that?'

It was a few hours before Harry could grab any spare time to go and investigate. He marched across the muddy furrows, waving to the land girls who were toiling higher up nearer the skyline and stopped by the fallen figure.

Their scarecrow, well Jake's really. He'd made more of him than Harry had. It was Jake who had stuffed the pillow case body with straw, used a sack for the head and drawn on a face. He'd even sewed on two buttons for the eyes and rescued their dad's old coat from the rag pile. Harry had performed the heavy lifting by tying the scarecrow up against the pole and hammering it upright into the ground. Harry was five years older and more muscular than Jake who was still a skinny stick of a boy.

The scarecrow was hanging half on, half off its pole. Lying at its straw feet was the huddled shape of a man. He was folded up, broken looking, filthy, but definitely a man who had obviously tried to grasp at the scarecrow's straw filled body to pull himself up, but failing he'd collapsed into the mud.

Harry bent down to shake the man's shoulder.

'Hey mister are you all right?' he asked.

Harry stopped talking though when he spotted what the mud had been hiding. The distinctive yellow edging around the grey outline of a shoulder patch, revealing a Luftwaffe cadet sergeant's strap badge. He'd only gone and found himself a bloody Kraut in his field!

Harry turned to shout over to the land girls to come and help, but then he shut his open mouth. He stood rigid, hands balled into fists hanging loosely. He thought instead of the baker Mr Thomas' son, who was never coming back. He thought of one of the land girls, sweet natured Elsie's fiancé, another non-returner and most painfully close to his heart, of his own father. Blown to pieces they'd heard and of the telegram which had arrived turning their guts to mush.

When these men had needed help who had been there for them? He thought of how young and scared Jake was under his fake toughness and of his mother who got up every day and went about her daily tasks in a trance. Her eyes dead, her lips squeezed thin and tight.

Harry took out his hankie and tore it into two strips. He tied one strip firmly over the soldier's mouth, gagging him and the other around his eyes. He made sure they were tightly knotted. Next he stripped the scarecrow and dressed the unconscious German soldier in his father's cast off trousers and coat.

Grunting with the effort Harry hauled up the heavy figure and covered the soldier's head in the burlap sack, leaving Jake's drawn on face with the button eyes to stare blindly out across the field. He bound the German with the same ropes which had been used to secure the scarecrow to the pole. He took especial care to ensure that the rope around the man's neck was tightly secured. Finally Harry scattered the left over straw and trampled it into the mud.

When he stepped back to inspect his handiwork, he was impressed. You really couldn't tell anything was amiss. Damn, it looked good, he thought.

The figure began to moan and wheeze. However blindfolded, gagged and trussed up like a turkey, the German had no chance of breaking free. His movements became more frenzied though Harry observed.

Harry strolled away jauntily whistling. He gave a parting wave in the direction of the land girls. He reckoned if he was lucky the German might last a day or so strapped up on the pole. Perhaps he would even pay him a visit later that night.

Love thy Neighbour

There had only been the two of them in the house when Alan had plunged to his death down the cellar steps, so everyone just assumed Alice had done it. Everyone on the street had known he'd used her like a rug to beat. Of course everyone was sorry. Sorry about her bruises, her black eyes, the arm in a pot. Not once but twice.

But you can't condone shoving your spouse to his death. Can you? However much of a bastard he was. Alice had to take her punishment. Justice had to be seen to be done. So it was prison for her. Nothing else for it. Done and dusted. Poor lass.

Course we all have our secrets. Some are little ones like Billy who lives three doors down, pinching money from his ma's purse when she's drunk.

You see poor timid Alice wasn't the only one. Alan's appetites were – varied shall we say?

I keep my own stash of x-rays with the spare key to his cellar door, secreted under my bedroom floorboards.

Alice and me are twins in a way. Which is why I visit her every month. Another secret.

Snow Man

You wear your waistcoat of ice so elegantly. Snow fell lightly in the night. It sits like sugar frosting on your suit. I've been watching you for hours through our bay window. Watched while the dusk came sipping at your toes, until complete darkness coated you in its chocolatey embrace.

Rose streaks the sky. I'm still here. So are you. A beautiful morning to wake into. I slurp my cold cup of coffee. It's time to make the call. Soon the winter rays will reveal the red stain on your chest.

My snow husband. Of frozen flesh and bloody ice.

Treasure Hunt

Our little gang of scavengers always take a vote before we head out. We're democratic that way.

That January day, the waste ground behind the newly built skyscraper won.

It was Billy who found the doll, lying in the frosty tipped grass. Weak sunshine gleamed on her glassy eyes.

Shoving it at me, Billy rubbed his hands on his denims, 'Yuk, it's slimy. Here Jem. You have it.'

None of us had toys, so this was real treasure.

Instantly I recognised it. From the 'Missing' posters pinned up around town.

The lost girl was cuddling it.

I kick it away.

Tomb Land

'The locals call it Tombland.'

'What locals? There's no one around for bloody miles.'

Liz gestures vaguely down the hillside to the village; a seam of cottages and a pub. You pull out your camera gear, the reason for this trip. Up on the moor you could easily imagine Heathcliff wandering around or a baying Hound of the Baskervilles. There's even a light mist rolling in.

'It's getting a bit Hammer horror up here love,' I say to her, pleading.

Liz ignores me, oblivious. This isn't unusual especially when she's framing a shot. To pacify my growing edginess I extract my pack of fags and take shelter alongside a mossy winged angel. In the match's brief spark I spot a lean shadow slip between the gravestones. Running and low slung to the ground. I blink and it's gone. Probably a stray dog I think. Still…

'You nearly done yet? That pub might be open.' I increase the pressure on Liz to wrap it up.

A bird nearby squawks. A brutal cry which is abruptly silenced. Now Liz is examining a vault door which is all carved curlicue metalwork. Pretty fancy looking, and expensive. These Victorians splashed their cash when it came to death and memorials.

'The lock's broken Pete. Take a look. Here.' Liz points her mitten.

'Could you be quiet?' I whisper.

I watch her turn, ready to argue. So I point in front and hold a finger to my lips. Loping down the grassy path towards us, surrounded by cherubs blowing their smothered trumpets, stalks a lean furry shape. Feral featured, whippet thin, with its muzzle smeared red and a broken feathery body hanging from it. Not a dog after all as I'd thought, but a wolf.

Panicked I push against the vault gate and it gives. We both squeeze through. The wolf paces closer, its amber eyes staring at us. Pulling the grille towards us, I secure it with my belt looped round.

'Great,' I mutter. 'We're locked in with the dead Liz. Hey would you stop taking photos?'

Liz is shooting images of the wolf's red frothy muzzle jammed up against the grille. He is agitated and focussed on us. She shrugs off my comment.

I turn away and descend the stone steps into the vault. Liz follows me a little reluctant to leave her wild animal photo op. Inside the vault there are stone shelves packed with wooden coffins. Further back there are a trio of raised stone steps leading up to a dais, where a large stone sarcophagus sits in solo majesty.

From behind the sarcophagus we can both hear a rustling, snuffling sound. We tense, holding our breaths. It's instinctive. Then we spot a furry snout peeking out somewhat cautiously. Next a tiny grey furred wolf cub follows the snout. Tumbling and gambolling happily.

This is no sanctuary. It is the wolf's den. I eye the coffins and nod at Liz.
'No,' she mouths.

I shrug. She can do what she pleases. Me I'm climbing inside one of those wooden boxes. Time to hide and consider my options. The dead can't hurt me after all.

The Last Walk

We saunter along the woodland trails, holding hands. The sky is heavy with snow, you heavy with our child. We've only just moved here, to this remote village. We are reborn. We have new names, new lives. Intoxicated, we revel in the luxury of time alone and together.

'I want to call her Hope,' I say as I stroke your distended belly.

We are safe here I tell myself. Though it occurs to me this lane is both private and at the same time, isolated. A blackbird bursts forth from the greenery. A harbinger.

Black garbed figures follow the bird. The bushes spew forth a quartet of young men.

I fight back. I always have. I always will. But I am overwhelmed by them. I feel their boots in my ribs, hear a crack of bone, taste salt on my lips. I suck in air, then swallow my own blood. I see you hooded, dragged away, kicking and wailing. You are becoming nothing but a dwindling dot disappearing down the lane. Exiting from our shared lives. Becoming history even as I lie there gasping. Your family have found us again. They always do.

Ride of a Lifetime

'Come on Harry you're not too old are you?'

Jim's tinted glasses glinted in the weak winter sunlight. Harry could see a tiny stunted version of himself reflected back.

He did not like what he saw. A thin, balding bloke with a worn creased face. Old before his time he thought. He knew who to blame for that too. She was draining him dry with her demands. He couldn't work or sleep and the bills were mounting. He'd be losing the house soon he guessed. When he'd had the text from Jim, a school mate from Beckfoot College days, Harry's heart had leapt. He'd remembered long boozy nights down the High Street, games of pool, fags and flutters on the horses. Fun. God how he'd missed that.

As young men everyone had said Harry and Jim were mirror images of each other. Both whippet-thin, wiry, fit, blonde hair, with a great sense of humour and lots of drive. Then they'd lost touch, just like that really or so Harry remembered it. He wasn't sure why.

It was Jim who'd resurrected Bridlington with all its youthful happy memories.

'Let's do it again Harry. Go back to our old stomping ground.'

Which was why two middle aged men, were during midwinter, loitering on Brid's sea front. Feeling the chill wind burn their cheeks and gazing up at the carousel with its silent brashly painted mounts.

Harry spoke up, 'It's bloody cold out here mate. Can't we head back to the pub?'

'Lighten up. Come on kill joy. I've got the keys. The owner's a pal of mine.'

Jim was heading off towards the start-up panel, keys jangling already out of his pocket. Typical thought Harry, Jim always knew someone. A trickle of resentment rolled over him.

Thirty years separated him from the spotty lad he had once been. Now he was a soon to be ex-Sales Manager, living in Hull with a mouthy soon to be ex-wife and two teenagers who barely acknowledged his existence but let him pay for everything. He simply didn't want to ride the funfair in bloody January. He wanted a warm fire, a pint and a sofa. Briefly he wondered again what, exactly Jim did for a job these days.

'Freelance.' Jim had said when Harry had asked him. In the pub he'd mentioned being in 'Quality control. Boring really mate.'

Harry turned to stare at the stormy grey waves, breaking over the beach. Like my life he thought bitterly. Behind him he heard the carousel gears grinding into life.

Jim was dangling off one of the horses, grinning broadly. 'Come on mate. All aboard.'

He looked fit and prosperous. Nothing like me then any more, thought Harry. He's kept his hair too. Lucky sod! We'd never be mistaken for twins now. He felt unaccountably sad about that.

Reluctantly Harry walked over and climbed aboard one of the bright red and gold horses, checking there was no one around to witness his idiocy. There was no one in sight. The front was totally deserted and Harry felt a frisson of anxiety.

The horses started speeding up, the lights were flashing, the music blaring out. Harry just felt sick and old. In the rotating central panel he could see himself in the spinning mirrors, a dozen Harrys. A dozen different lives he could have lived.

Jim was shouting 'Gee up!' He was two horses behind Harry.

Harry heard nothing, until he felt strong fingers grab at his neck in a choke hold and he smelt Jim's beery breath on his face.

'What the f…?' Harry mumbled, struggling and still watching himself in the carousel mirrors. Jim was on his back, almost riding him. He heard him say, 'Bye Harry. Your number's up mate.'

Sharp pain flooded Harry's right side. Glancing down he saw a red stain bloom on his fleece jumper. Wobbling he tried to grab onto Jim, whose face was strangely calm, almost blank. Nothing showed in it at all. Just a tiny crease between his eyebrows.

'Just a job, sorry Harry. I'm being paid to get rid of inferior product. Which in this case is you.'

Harry slumped over his horse, his torso covering its gilt mane.

The music played for another minute or so then the carousel ground to a halt. Light feathers of snow began to fall. A gentle cloak lying over Harry's shoulders as though to keep him warm.

Jim checked his own appearance in the carousel mirror, sweeping back his hair. He liked to look smart. It mattered how you looked. Once it had been like looking in a mirror looking at Harry. Not now though. His old mate had really let himself go.

He patted Harry's shoulder. 'See ya around mate.'

He didn't mean to be ironic. That wasn't in his make up. Jim jumped down and sauntered off, looking like a man without a care in the world.

Crowd Control

The crowds heaved and surged. They were all waiting, waiting for Him to appear. The darkness was spasmodically torn apart by neon slashes from the state of the art lighting system. Meanwhile the noise levels hit new peaks. When the star finally strutted onto the stage in his black leathers, the audience's frenzy burst out unrestrained.

'Like a million coke cans detonated at once,' said Jake. 'He's an hour late, we've paid for this and we're still supposed to be grateful. All he has to do is sing. Some of us have real work to do here tonight.'

This venue, this gig, hadn't really been his choice. Rather Lisa had bought the tickets, booked the date in the diary and arranged it all. As always. Great little organiser was his Lisa. He was lucky to have her. Well so he'd been told by her and her family often enough.

The star draped the microphone over his silver-studded shoulders, climbed over the piano and pranced in front of the huge screens, beginning to give his money's worth. Jake watched, indifferent to the display. He kept checking his watch. Timing was everything this evening.

Lisa snuggled into his shoulder and breathed in his smell happily. What a night! She couldn't wait to get home and post the photo of the ring on Facebook. That would show them all! All those bitchy cows at the office and down at the pub who said Jake would never settle, never commit.

'Wasting your time darlin' you know. It's not his style. New girl every other month or so. His mum was the same. More fellas than hot dinners.'

Lisa stroked the sparkler on her left hand. Okay, she guessed it was probably fake or at best nicked. But she wasn't going to ask too many questions. It didn't really matter. She'd got the ring out of him when no other girl had. It was bloody loud up here though, right at the back. Hot too. Crowded in like sardines.

'Darling can you move your arm a bit I'm getting hot,' she spoke right into Jake's ear. He didn't reply.

Lisa tried to shrug off Jake's hand but instead his grip on her shoulder tightened and then moved up to her throat. He had large hands, hairy too, she'd always thought that. He kept staring ahead as well. Now he was squeezing, tighter. She began to choke, but it came out like a whimper. No one would hear with all this noise around her.

Under siege she gasped and tried to wriggle free. No one looked over at her. They were all entranced by the huge screens and the images displayed on them or intent on holding up their iPhones or taking selfies.

Lisa felt her vision narrow to flickering white dots then blackness. Jake held her firmly erect in his embrace. Her head lolled as if affectionately on his shoulder.

Silly cow, he thought. They all were though.

No one noticed, no one looked his way, not even when Jake got up to leave an hour or so into the gig. Dressed in anonymous black, he melted into the shadows at the back of the arena, slipping from the building into the Yorkshire night air.

Laughter in the Dark

"If you're going to tell people the truth, be funny or they'll kill you."

Billy Wilder

3D Audrey

The tube doors smacked shut behind the slim brunette in the green coat, trapping Audrey Hepburn's head in the gap. Ebbonnie struggled and tussled. Her handbag had her in a choke hold around her neck. The doors snapped hungrily again. Open. Closed. This time they nibbled Audrey's tiara.

With a final tug Ebbonnie wrested the life size cardboard figure inside the carriage and fell back against a seat. Audrey, in her little black dress, stood propped drunkenly against a window. She looked perfectly groomed, whereas Ebbonnie was a sweaty mess.

'Got your hands full there love.'

The bloke opposite smiled. He has nice eyes Ebbonnie thought, on auto pilot, not really interested. Not since the Darren fiasco.

'What are you doing carrying her around?'

He nodded at Audrey, his mouth crinkling.

'It's for my boss's party. Part of the deck core.'

Tube Guy looked a bit confused. Then he laughed, 'Oh right. Funny.'

Ebbonnie wondered what he meant. She glanced out of the window, 'Nearly my stop. Hammersmith. Gotta go.'

Struggling she tried to haul Audrey upright. Audrey resisted.

'Here let me give you a hand. It's not often you get to grips with one of your idols. I'd have 'Breakfast at Tiffany's' with her any day.' He laughed heartily, so Ebbonnie being polite, smiled back.

Tube Guy firmly grabbed Audrey by the waist and spun her expertly around, making it look easy.

The train halted.

'Do you fancy going to see her in 3D then?' asked Tube Guy, smiling at both Ebbonnie and Audrey. 'She's showing at the BFI. They've got a season of her films. We could OD on Audrey.'

More flashing teeth.

Ebbonnie couldn't help admiring Tube Guy's muscle definition in his T-shirt. She didn't want to admit that a 'Police Academy' was more her type of film. She'd never heard of Audrey Hepburn either. But she'd Google her later.

Ebbonnie followed Tube Guy and Audrey out onto the platform watching while he stood posing with his arm around Audrey's waist taking a selfie. She had to admit they were a perfect match. She didn't know how she could compete with his screen dream girl. Not that Tube Guy seemed to want Ebbonnie in the shot anyway.

It had been a long day. Carting this cardboard figure on and off the Tube had been a nightmare of a job. Ebbonnie's feet throbbed. Her tights were snagged and her nail polish chipped. She didn't feel very friendly towards Audrey at that moment. Tube Guy's charms were wearing a bit thin too.

'Perhaps you could take er… 'Audrey' round to my boss's address?'

Ebbonnie handed Tube Guy a card.

'He'll be ever so thrilled. I'll follow in a taxi. There wouldn't be room for the three of us in one cab.'

'Great idea.' Tube Guy beamed.

Ebbonnie watched him trot off, Audrey slung under his arm. She sighed heavily and headed in the opposite direction towards the nearest 'Be At One' bar.

Peacocks

The tall hungry looking girl and the bird were being photographed together against the terracotta stone backdrop of the 17th century manor house. One was the focus, the other was the prop. One was all glamour, draped in aquamarine chiffon; the other was pecking in vituperation at the gravel.

'Amazing darling. Hold that pose. Give me more hair. Fuller lips. Great! Pull your top down a bit lovey.'

The skinny photographer leapt around like a hyperactive spider. Around him, a tiny (but essential) entourage hovered, keeping out of both birds' way. They had all learnt early on that morning where the safe zone was.

A maze of birdseed decorated the patio; it served as a lure for the peacock, with only partial success. The bird did his own thing. The model, who hadn't eaten in hours, kept eyeing the seeds hungrily. She was trying to work out how many calories there were in maize. The peacock drifted nearer to the valuable chiffon gown.

The model, nervous, on edge, shrieked, 'Keep that bloody bird away from me can't you?'

'Think Karma darling, think Zen thoughts.' The photographer babbled on. 'Lift your arms, like you're going to fly.'

Obediently the model lifted her stick thin limbs so that the chiffon fabric would appear wing-like, and would blow gauzily in the breeze. Just for a moment all was a vision of glorious aquamarine and turquoise glimmering in the sunshine.

The peacock, plunged in urgent forward momentum, aiming for the only bit of fat on the model, her juicy big toe, which was protruding from the sliver of shoes priced at several thousand.

Screams split the air, 'Ow! It got me! That damn bird bit me! I'm going to need antibiotics in case I catch Ebola.'

There was some sniggering among the tiny entourage at that outburst.

'Great shot though darling, with you leaping up like that. Very energised.' The photographer commented. It was part of his job to stay calm.

The peacock, by now totally fed up with the carnival unfolding in his private domain, pulled in his own aquamarine cloak and mooched away to find his more tolerant mate.

Zombie Hunting

We're sitting in a hide in the middle of Dalby Forest all weaponed up, in camouflage gear. Me and Lisa and the rest of our zombie hunter team mates. It's pitch black but not silent. We keep hearing screams and howls coming from out of the trees.

Lisa has arranged this as a Valentine's present for us. I had been hoping to just exchange cards.

We've been a couple for five years but I've not proposed, so I know Lisa is getting a bit edgy.

'It'll be a fun, bonding thing. Spend the night fighting side by side like in "The Walking Dead",' she'd wheedled.

'Come on guys let's get out there!' Lisa says. No one moves.

I stand up. I have to go with her.

It's pretty creepy in the woods. The website's photos of the zombies are totally convincing. I'm jumping at shadows like a kid again, holding up my semi-automatic air soft rifle in front of me.

Looking like an extra from "World War Z" a figure comes streaking out at us. All white body paint, red mouth and fast. Very fast. Not like a human at all.

Lisa gets off a few shots and the zombie drops writhing to the earth.

'Fantastic' she shouts.

We move together, shoulder to shoulder, high on adrenalin now.

'I love you Lisa,' I whisper.
'Do you?' she replies.
Another figure comes howling towards us.
I scream and shove Lisa in front me. 'Take her!' I yell.

Vinnie's Family

It's date night for me and Vinnie. He's brought me to his family crypt. He's a bit of a Goth is Vin.

Wears skull rings and black eye makeup. Dances to his own tune. Rides this amazing motorbike too. Inside we cuddle in rather close propinquity to his ancestors.

He's brought some red wine for us to drink. So I am feeling no pain having drunk more than my share. Floppy and relaxed I lean against him. I'm fairly certain he's going to propose. I imagine a diamond ring or maybe a ruby, because Vinnie does like the colour red. His whole bedroom is done out in red and black. He wears red satin boxers.

Vinnie lies me gently down on a tomb's lid, arranging me carefully. He's such a gentleman.

Then he steps away from me and turns towards the back wall where two large fancy wooden coffins are propped up.

'Mum! Dad! Dinner's served.'

What did he say? I try to sit upright but I'm too sozzled.

The two coffin lids lift up. Their inhabitants step out or rather float towards me. They are not the sort of in-laws I expected.

Life Scenes

"Reality continues to ruin my life."
        Bill Watterson, The Complete Calvin and Hobbes

Cannon Fodder

The gnawing started as soon as night fell; incisors clicking, feet scurrying over both the dead and live bodies indiscriminately. The rats feasted. There wasn't much you could do about it. The living had nowhere to escape to anyway. Their living quarters were awash with mud, corpses and spent bullet cases. There was no colour anywhere in these French fields. The landscape was an unadulterated brown. Its horizons punctuated by wire fences. At night the blackness was rent by the sound of men's moaning.

Private Bill Mason sucked heavily on his cigarette. Huddled down in his trench, he was soaked through. The lice made his scalp itch. It had been a day to end all days – a living hell. The enemy's Howitzers had hammered away for hours. Mason's ears rang, constantly.

He didn't know what to write home. There were no words to describe what his life had become. Writing and words had never been his strength, instead he'd been good at making things.

Bloody useless in this war though, he thought. When all any man could do was watch everything and everyone be pulverised.

'My dearest Lily… It is night now. I can see hundreds of stars. It is quiet enough. I miss you, your cooking, our…'

Mason absent-mindedly rubbed his right foot. The stub of his big toe buzzed, with phantom energy. He'd lost it a few months back. Frostbite, gangrene, the usual. He was lucky though he knew. It was just his toe. So far. He felt his eyes fill. He swallowed hard.

You had to get a hold of feelings, else they'd be your undoing. He'd seen men dragged away, gibbering.

'When I get home Lily, I'm going to make you that dresser you always wanted.'

Mason contemplated the planing of the hardwood under his hands. Recalled he wood's smell and his Lily's face.

He would not think about tomorrow.

Going Home

Shattered glass crunched under her bare feet and bit into her flesh. The blood matched her toenail varnish. Lucia barely noticed. In her head all she could see, indeed smell, was her mother's cooking. The spices she associated with love.

    It had been a long walk home. The last two miles of it she had trodden, blood-shod. The passing verbal assaults from random truck drivers had barely registered. Her husband doled out worse, as her daily diet.

    Lucia ignored the signs stating 'Due for Demolition', ducking under the tape she curled up on her mother's living room floor and slept. Safe.

No Home for Holly

Holly had been searching for her mother for years. In every hostel, shelter and B&B she moored at she would investigate every room. The voices told her where to look and also when to leave. Though more often than not her relentless searching was the cause of her being evicted, again and again.

Holly had got accustomed to the name calling. 'Crazy girl!' 'Fruity loops.' 'Holly's off her trolley.' These were among the gentler epithets.

The violence she experienced though always shocked her; disconnecting her from her inner radar. Leaving her anchorless.

Mikey wasn't like that. He was both street-wise and street-damaged. The day he'd met Holly he'd disinterred her from the grubby bowels of the dumpsters behind Asda, where she'd fallen in. She'd been skip diving and whilst scrabbling to climb out had cut her leg. The gash was deep; this wound was visible.

The trip to A&E had been a savage assault on her senses – a white walled noisy hell. It hummed of antiseptic and old vomit. Holly had found it hard to cope. Shaking she'd clung to Mikey's arm. He kept the voices at bay.

The hospital still had the remnants of some tatty tinsel up. Under the forgotten mistletoe twig in the A&E was where Mikey gave her their first kiss.

After the kiss he told her he'd got a spot selling the 'Big Issue'. He'd help her try for the gig too. Put in a word. They could hang out together.

'Just for now and the near tomorrows. If it's what you'd like Holly.'

Holly put her hand in his and felt his scars rub against hers.

'We could be each other's home,' she whispered.

Bookworm

Grandad's library overspilled with valuable tomes. There were towers of toppling treatises; dens to be constructed with just his encyclopaedias alone. You could lose yourself in this labyrinth of lexicons. Certainly a skinny shy child of less than ten years could hide away there. Forgotten and forgetting herself.

Looking back, whole weeks of my childhood summers evaporated, ensconced among his first editions. My hands smelt of leather and ink. Every day I would sniff them ecstatically before washing them in readiness for teatime.

I had my favourites of course. A nineteenth century world atlas, hand coloured. A child's speller from World War 2. Grandad's privately published monographs on the family history with my name penned in black italics.

One rainy day Grandad handed me a beautifully wrapped square package.

'For you Ali.'

This was a rare treat indeed. Grandad did not give gifts wantonly. He remembered war time rationing.

'This is the most valuable book you will ever own,' he told me.

Hands shaking, I unwrapped the package, pocketing the purple velvet ribbon to reuse. Inside lay a small, rather plain book with empty pages. It rather resembled me at that age.

'There's nothing in it Grandad.' I said. At ten years old you are very literal as I recall.

'It is your first diary. For you to write whatever record of your life you wish to remember. It will be priceless to you one day.'

When years later he died, Grandad bequeathed me his library in all its splendour. The diary resides within its walls. With each rereading my memory tree grows new leaves.

Visiting Mum

She's such a nice girl. The one with the red hair, always smiling at me. She chats while she combs my hair, buttons my cardigan, hands me my walker frame and tucks a hand under my arm, helping me up. I notice her nails are shiny black, as if they've been caught in a door. Has she had an accident?

'There we go Mrs Carlton. Let's get you into the day room.'

Her words soothe our fractured progress. Stop start. Stop start. The room looks murky and unfamiliar.

'Have I been here before?' I hear myself ask. I am shocked at the sound of my voice. It is so old. Is that really me speaking? I glance at the girl to see if she's shocked. But no, she's still smiling.

'Yes it's the day lounge.'

She moves my walker away. I feel a stab of anxiety.

'No.'

'Don't worry it'll be just here.' She pats the frame. 'Your son is coming soon.'

Looking around I spy two other huddled shapes sitting in chairs. One is lightly snoring. Who are they? I sense that I should know. It is like being in a grey fog.

A shadow blocks out my light, 'Hello Ma.'

A tall man bends down to kiss my cheek. He smells cleanly of soap. 'How are you today?'

The curtains flutter and open. 'Darling boy, how lovely to see you.'

I smile at him, irresistibly drawn to his features. So like someone else's I once knew. Of course – it's Robert, my eldest.

'I'll just get a pot of tea sorted for us Ma.'

He pours the tea into the cup and hands it to me. I take it carefully. The china feels so thin. Like bones. I worry it will break. I don't know where to put it. I start to get anxious.

I must pay attention. Robert's chatting to me.

'I took the boys snowboarding the other day Ma. They're getting really good now. Josh loves the climbing wall too.'

His voice saunters on, wrapping me in its soft rhythms. I feel comforted. I have found somewhere to put the cup. Silence falls.

'Ma where's your cup of tea gone?'

I panic. What does he mean? Am I in trouble?

Robert bends down and sighing, picks up something from under the stool.

'Oh here it is Ma. Drink it before it gets cold.'

I sip at it, tasting only sodden tea towels. I don't like it. I don't want it.

'Robbie take it away. Please. Can you? Now.'

His face is huge beside me. He towers over me. I am shrinking. Silence again, except for the snoring in the corner and the buzz of the light bulb. The cup is gone now. I feel fingers touch my hand. My skin is like old paper I think. My head starts to droop.

When I wake the curtains are drawn, the lamps on the corner tables are lit. I am alone. I am not sure where I am. I am so small, in this huge chair. What if no one ever comes?

A young girl comes up to me. She has a nice smile and red hair. Her fingernails are black. Has she hurt herself I wonder?

'Was there someone here?' I ask her.

'Yes, your son came to see you Mrs Carlton. Like he does every Sunday. Come on let's get you up.'

She pulls my walker towards me. I grasp the metal bars gratefully. It is familiar. It is a friend.

MISPER

In my cousin's lounge, awash with middle class emblems, there are two factions at war. The neutral space is the hallway, so I hover there. I am undecided. Do I turn west into the lounge or east into the kitchen. Each compass point brings its own problems.

I am coltishly young, unassertive, educated but unschooled too. There are, I realise that day, huge lacunas in my knowledge of my family's history.

No one is explaining why at my Aunt Em's funeral, her two daughters refuse to share the air with their father, my uncle.

No one explains either why he wanders around, my dear uncle, with trembling fingers enveloping his whiskey glass, smiling amiably but blankly at everyone. There is no one at home in his head anymore. Where has he gone to? He is at sea in his daughter's home.

From the kitchen an exotically accented voice rises, a direct contrast to the Yorkshire damp and gloam of this February funeral day.

'He killed her. Ma soeur est morte à cause de cet homme!' – *My sister is dead because of that man.*

There follows a cacophony of hushing and crying entwined.

The words shock. I freeze. I understand the translation but not their meaning. How can my uncle be guilty of this? Aunt Em died, horrendously of cancer which laid her waste in months.

I watch the dust-motes dancing in a ray of sun leaking through the stained glass in the front door. I am, I realise, still standing in the hallway.

My uncle ambles past ever present glass in hand. He is smiling at no one as is his wont.

'Nice day isn't it? So lovely to see everyone. Where did I put my cigs?'

I grab his arm, 'Don't go into the kitchen Uncle.'

Some instinct has gripped me. I have to spare him. He is old. Adrift. I love him. He is my mother's only brother.

I say, 'Here let's go sit in the lounge. Come with me.'

Like a child he follows me. I steer him onto the sofa. I seat him next to my mother, who adores him unconditionally, as she has always done.

For the moment he is safe.

Epilogue

"She gave me a smile I could feel in my hip pocket."

Raymond Chandler

Dames and Rain Slicked Streets (Riff to Film Noir)

She sashayed into my office, all pout, bee stung lips and a hank of hair and a stream of wisecracks. We smart talked back and forth for a few minutes to break the ice. It was getting dark outside, only the neon sign "JOE's BAR" strobed my office. I flicked my table lamp on. She leant into the orange circle and asked me for a light. Her lips were so dark they looked blood stained. She was the sort of woman who came alive at night.

Her pencil skirt hugged her hips as she came around my desk edge as she bent down towards my silver lighter. I breathed in her scent, Lily of the Valley. But she was no Lily. Not her.

'I want you to find my sister,' she whispered. I felt her breath on my cheek.

'Where did you lose her?' I asked. I couldn't help myself.

'Funny guy huh?' She lightly slapped my cheek and taking the lighter off me, walked over to the window. I watched the blue and red letters flicker on and off across her lean figure. She looked like a greyhound. A neon greyhound.

'Will you help me?' She turned towards me, her hair covering one eye.

Her beret pulled down low.

'I'm a helpful kind of guy. For $100 up front I'll play ball.'

She pouted. I felt a bead of sweat run down my back. 'My baby sister is our daddy's favourite. He can't bear she's gone.'

'Aren't you anyone's favourite?'

She took a pull on her cigarette, shrugged but didn't reply. Looking out of my window she suddenly stiffened.

'They've followed me. Damn. I thought I'd shaken them off.'

I almost believed her. She was good I'd give her that.

'Who?' Playing along.

'Mr Desiree's hired goons. Out there.'

I knew that name. Everyone in town knew Desiree. He was into everything. Girls, dope, gambling. I got up and went to stand beside her. She was almost my height. I like that in a woman. I like her to match me. Her hair brushed my shoulder.

'See there. In the black Buick.' She nodded outside the rain smeared glass.

There was a black Buick parked opposite and there were two heavy looking guys in the front seat. Looked kind of strange the pair of them sitting like that as if they were on a date or something. Maybe she was right. I'd give her the benefit of the doubt. She was worth it.

'OK.'

I walked over to my desk drawer, opened it and pulled out my gun. It felt familiar.

She grabbed my arm, 'What are you going to do?'

'Go out and have a little chat with them. Isn't that what you're paying me for?'

'I haven't paid you anything yet,' she replied gazing right into my eyes. Hers were green like a cats. I don't know what colour mine are. Blood shot probably.

'Well we can sort that out when I come back.'

'What if you don't?' she whispered right by my mouth. Then she lifted her lips, her dark lips, and kissed me. She tasted of cigarettes and whisky. My kind of taste.

'I'll be back,' I said. I had a lot to come back for now.

Pulling on my raincoat, it's always raining in this damn city, I headed out into the night to face – well who knew? What I did know was she was lying her head off, but I also knew for certain she was a helluva broad.

Acknowledgements of prior publication for Flash Fiction pieces

Children's Games has appeared in Raging Aardvark's anthology *Twisted Tales 2016*; also on www.etherbooks.com as a downloadable story; and in *A Cache of Flashes* published by Black Pear Press (as the winners in Worcestershire Literature Festival Flash Fiction Competition 2016).

A Gift for Krampus has appeared in *Three Drops from a Cauldron* Midwinter 2016 anthology and on DigitalFictionPub.com as part of their *QuickFic edition 5*.

Mother Love was first published on www.101words.org, as a reprint on www.philslattery.wordpress.com and in the *Violet Hour Journal* October 2016 issue.

Nest of Bones was short-listed and published on www.404words.com (a now archived website)

The Wake Up Call first appeared on www.thedrabble.wordpress.com, then as a reprint on www.philslattery.wordpress.com.

Mermaid on the Ad Hoc Fiction flash fiction site: http://adhocfiction.com, and an 80-word version on www.third-word.com where it won 1st prize in the monthly competition.

All Hallows' Eve is included in Otley Writers' Group self-published anthology October 2017 *The Darkening Season*.

The Adelphi (a similar version) has appeared on https://horrortree.com/category/trembling-with-fear. (Later in an anthology edited by Stuart Conover.)

Cathedral Crow won 1st place on www.zeroflash.wordpress.com monthly competition in June 2016. It also appeared on www.ironsoap.com (both the site and an anthology) and as a reprint on www.threedropspoetry.co.uk in issue 7 of their web journal in November 2016.

Belladonna has been published on *Three Drops from the Cauldron* web journal issue 14 in March 2017.

Chestnuts for my Sweet was published on www.thecasket.co.uk.

Doll Man was first published on www.thecasket.co.uk and is included in Otley's Writers' anthology *The Pulse of Everything*.

A Guy for the Children first appeared on Morgen Bailey's blog as the winner of her November 2015 monthly competition, as a reprint on www.thedrabble.wordpress.com, and in *The Pulse of Everything* anthology.

Snow Man appeared on www.thedrabble.wordpress.com the Ad Hoc Fiction flash fiction site: http://adhocfiction.com.

Treasure Hunt was 1st prize winner on Helen Yendall's blog in June 2016.

The Last Walk first appeared on www.200wordtuesdays.blogspot.co.uk.

3D Audrey has been published by www.etherbooks.com as a downloadable story for iPhones.

Peacocks first appeared on http://www.funnyinfivehundred.com and is available as a podcast on iTunes.

Zombie Hunting appeared on www.postcardshorts.com/read-2552.html.

Cannon Fodder was one of twelve winning entries for the TubeFlash 2016 Flash Fiction competition run by www.thecasket.co.uk in conjunction with BBC Arts Get Creative; it is available as a download from Apple iTunes. It also appears in the anthology *The Pulse of Everything*, and as a reprint on Calum Kerr's blog www.flashfloodjournal.blogspot.co.uk as part of National Flash Fiction Day 2017.

No Home for Holly appeared on www.zeroflash.org and won a 'Special Mention.'

Also By Chapeltown Books

Spectrum
by Christopher Bowles

A collection of one hundred and ten pieces of flash-fiction and poetry. You probably won't like all of them, and some of them might even disgust you, or make you uncomfortable. But stick with it. Look at overarching themes within each coloured block. Find the puns in certain titles. Research the colours that you've never heard of. Try and work out which stories are complete fabrications, which ones contain nuggets of truth, and which ones are versions of real life events.

Order from Amazon:
ISBN: 978-1-910542-13-2 (paperback)
978-1-910542-14-9 (ebook)

Chapeltown Books

Fog Lane
by Neil Campbell

Fog Lane is a collection of stories about memory. Many of the stories have been published online and in magazines. They were written over a long period of time. The oldest, *The Rose Garden* was first written in about 2007 and published in Orbis. The last one in the book, *Here Comes the Sun*, was completed in 2017. The stories in this book vary from the humorous to the sad to the macabre. They are all short stories of under a thousand words.

Order from Amazon:

ISBN: 978-1-910542-08-8 (paperback)

978-1-910542-09-5 (ebook)

Chapeltown Books

January Stones
by Gill James

These stories were written one a day throughout January 2013. They were originally published on a blog called Gill's January Stones. Sometimes the stories would come right at the beginning of the day. Sometimes they would take a while longer.

Do they have a theme? Not really, though the idea of 'stones' is one of turning them over slowly on the beach until we find the right one.

There was no strict word count. Each story is as long as it needs to be. It had to be finished, though, by midnight of that day.

Order from Amazon:
ISBN: 978-1-910542-10-1 (paperback)
978-1-910542-11-8 (ebook)

Chapeltown Books

By James Nash, poet and tutor of Otley WEA Writers

Cinema Stories

Before the Second World War there were around seventy cinemas operating in Leeds. Now, though some remain open, most of these 'forgotten temples' have been repurposed or demolished. Since 2014, Leeds-based poets James Nash and Matthew Hedley Stoppard have been visiting the sites of legendary picture-houses, and documenting their current status with two inimitable, unmistakable poetic voices – whilst also considering the remarkable shared (yet personal) experience that is cinema-going.

Order from Amazon:
ISBN: 978-1-908853-52-3 (paperback)
ASIN: B0198J9R4I (ebook)